Hunter's Best Friend at School

By Laura Malone Elliott

Illustrations by Lynn Munsinger

SCHOLASTIC INC.

New York Toronto London Auckland Sydney
Mexico City New Delhi Hong Kong Buenos Aires

For Peter and Megan
–L.M.E.

For James, Brandy, and Krissy
–L.M.

ISBN 0-439-58933-9

Text copyright © 2002 by Laura Malone Elliot.
Illustrations copyright © 2002 by Lynn Munsinger. All rights reserved.
Published by Scholastic Inc., 557 Broadway, New York, NY 10012,
by arrangement with HarperCollins Publishers.
SCHOLASTIC and associated logos are trademarks
and/or registered trademarks of Scholastic Inc.

12 11 10 9 8 7 6 5 4 3 2 1   3 4 5 6 7 8/0

Printed in the U.S.A.   40

First Scholastic printing, October 2003

Typography by Al Cetta

Hunter and Stripe were best friends. They liked all the same things.

Hunter liked to wear striped sweaters. So did Stripe.

Hunter loved to somersault. Stripe did, too.

Hunter's favorite story was *Goldilocks and the Three Raccoons*. So was Stripe's. They even liked the same lunch: a crawfish sandwich, huckleberries, and milk.

At school Hunter and Stripe did everything together. On the playground Stripe pushed Hunter on the swing. Then Hunter pushed Stripe. When Stripe tried a cartwheel, Hunter did, too.

They drove the pretend school bus and sang, "The wheels
on the bus go round and round." And most days they'd
end recess by chasing Luna around the jungle gym. She
could run faster than either of them.

One day Stripe came to school in a mischief-making
mood. At circle time, he kept squirming and poking Hunter.
Their teacher, Mr. Ringtail, was reading a very interesting
book about ladybugs. But Hunter hardly heard any of it.

During snack, Stripe stuck out his tongue. At first it seemed funny, so Hunter did, too. But the other raccoon children didn't like seeing Stripe's half-eaten grasshopper.

"Yuck," Luna squealed. "Mr. Ringtail, Hunter and Stripe are making me sick!"

"Hunter, Stripe," said Mr. Ringtail, "you two can't sit
next to each other if you're going to do that."
He made them sit apart. Hunter was sad.

In art the class made paper frogs. Hunter loved to paint and color. But cutting with scissors along a line was hard for him. He snipped carefully, especially around the webbed feet.

When he was almost done, he heard Stripe laughing. Hunter looked over at him.

Stripe was hopping up and down and cutting his frog into shreds. He threw the little pieces of paper up into the air so that they fell in a shower over him. All the raccoons at Stripe's table were giggling.

"Whoopee! Look at me, Hunter," Stripe called. "This is fun. Come on, Hunter."

Hunter gazed proudly at his frog. He really wanted to finish it and color in big, googly eyes and paste on a long tongue. His mom would love it. She'd tape it on his closet door.

"Come on, Hunter," Stripe yelled again.

Hunter started dancing. He chopped up his frog and shouted, "Whoopee!" But when his frog lay all over the floor in scraps, Hunter felt awful. His beautiful frog was ruined. One big tear ran down his snout.

"Hunter," asked Mr. Ringtail, "was this your best work?"

Hunter looked down at his feet. "No," he said.

Mr. Ringtail thought a moment. Then he said, "Let's pick up the pieces and put them in your backpack."

The rest of the day was terrible. Stripe acted mad at
Hunter. Luna didn't want to be chased on the playground.

When Hunter got home, he tried to sneak his backpack
into his bedroom. But his mom saw him as he reached the
stairs. "Let's see what you've brought home today," she said.

Hunter handed her his pack. "What's this?" she asked as all the scraps of paper fell to the floor.

Hunter told his mom about Stripe and chopping up his frog. He left out the part about the half-eaten grasshopper and sticking out his tongue.

"Hmmmm," she said. "I understand the problem, Hunter. You like going along with your friend, right?"

Hunter nodded. "We do everything together."

"But you need to do what your teacher asks, right?"

Hunter nodded again.

"Do you feel good about chopping up your frog?"

"No," Hunter said sadly.

His mom hugged him. "You know what? I bet Stripe doesn't feel good about acting so silly either. Being a best friend doesn't mean always following along. Sometimes being a best friend means you have to help your friend be his best self."

The next day Hunter worried all the way to school. What if Stripe acted up again?

At circle time, Stripe lay flat on the floor and rolled back and forth as Mr. Ringtail read a book about turtles. Hunter thought about copying his friend. But he knew he really didn't want to.

So Hunter frowned at Stripe. He tried to make his eyebrows go up and his mouth go down like his grandfather sometimes did to make him be quiet at the library. But Stripe just laughed.

Then Stripe started tickling Hunter. Hunter turned
purple trying not to giggle. He scooched out of Stripe's
reach. He sat very, very still and listened to the story.
Maybe Stripe would copy *him*, thought Hunter.

After a minute, Stripe sat up, too. Mr. Ringtail smiled.

During snack, Stripe tried to toss his minnow fish across
the room into Mr. Ringtail's coffee cup. One of them stuck
on the window.

Hunter ignored him, even when Stripe landed a fish
on his head. "I can make an *M* with my minnows," Hunter
said to Luna.

Stripe stopped to watch Hunter. Then he made an *F*
for *fish* with his minnows before eating them carefully,
one by one.

While Mr. Ringtail set up finger painting, Stripe stuck
his right paw in some blue paint and his left paw in some
yellow paint. Then he crept up behind Luna. He whispered
to Hunter that he was going to make two paw prints on
Luna's perfectly clean dress.

"Wait!" Hunter cried. "Look what I can do, Stripe."
Hunter slapped his paws on paper to mix red and blue
together. They made purple.

"Cool," said Stripe. "What will mine make?" He rubbed the blue and yellow on his paper.

"Green," they said together.
"That's my favorite color," said Luna.

The rest of the day Stripe was his very best self. He helped Mr. Ringtail clean up after art.

He led the hunt for Luna's lost bracelet and found it behind her cubby.

He sat perfectly still next to Hunter as the music teacher taught them to sing, "This raccoon, he played one. . . ."

Out in the playground, Stripe and Hunter ran and cartwheeled and somersaulted and chased Luna around and around, just like always. Luna even let Hunter catch her, just this once.

That afternoon, as Hunter and Stripe sat waiting for their moms on the school's front steps, Stripe reached over and hugged Hunter.

"Hunter," Stripe told him, "you're my best friend."